# Hopscotch and the Case of the

# Missing Memories

By Kara Mugleston

To Flick and Jules—

May you always find a friend in a book

**Chapter 1**

My tail thumped against the hardwood floor as I waited patiently for my breakfast. Camilla, eleven years old with fire-red hair, flipped over the bacon and pancakes. Drew, her twin brother, plopped down at the breakfast table. His pant leg had rolled itself halfway up his calf in his sleep.

Their father, Mr. Walker, studied a case file while munching on his toast. His detective badge gleamed in the morning light.

"Since I've got you both here . . ." he started, forgetting about me. He was always doing that. "There's a new case I'm working on. I can't give you any details," he added, seeing Drew's mouth open in a question, "but I want you two to stay close to home, stay out of trouble, and stay together."

"Can't you give us a hint, Dad?" Drew whined.

"You know I can't. Not until this thing is wrapped up. Once this case is closed, I'll give you all the details." He pressed a kiss to each of their heads, said goodbye, then walked out the door.

It didn't escape my notice that he didn't say goodbye to me.

After our traditional breakfast, and after Drew got dressed, Drew and Camilla wheeled their bikes from the garage. Drew had thoughtfully added a basket on the back of his bike to allow me to ride on. For some reason, he thought that since I only had three legs, I couldn't run. I never bothered to tell him otherwise.

Drew hoisted me up into the metal basket. "You're getting heavy," he muttered under his breath. I hung my head. It's true that my stomach was getting rounder, and it was getting harder to climb the stairs, but I was missing a leg, and my chances for exercise were limited, with Drew

3

thinking I couldn't run. Plus, Camilla cooked bacon every morning, not that I minded.

I dug into the blanket until it comfortably surrounded me. Once I was settled, we took off to the park. We did it regularly, and I loved my naps in the shade while the twins played.

Today, though, things changed.

## Chapter 2

"I think I found something," Camilla said. She bent down and picked up something brown and square. It had been well hidden by the overgrown grass.

I lifted my head lazily and sniffed the air. Hmm. It smelled faintly of chlorine, with a hint of sweat. Nothing interesting.

Drew, however, thought it was interesting. "Is that a wallet? Is there any money in there?"

Camilla's red hair whipped around as she gave him a disdainful look. "This is not finder's keepers. We are not keeping the wallet. We need to give it back."

I got up from my spot in the shade and hobbled over. The sun baked into my yellow fur, heating up my body. Examining the wallet closer, I saw that it was well used, maybe a hand-me-down, but not thick. There definitely wasn't a lot of money in there, if any.

"I don't see a driver's license or anything. Oh, but there's a library card." Camilla pulled it out. "Hmm. No name on it. Maybe Mrs. Johnson can tell us who it belongs to."

I wrinkled my nose, and Drew let out a groan. It was no secret we didn't like the library, and the library didn't like us.

"No, let's just leave it here. The owner will come back for it, I'm sure," Drew reasoned.

"Not if they don't know it's here. Come on. The library isn't far. Besides, I need to return my books." She strode over to the bikes.

"Dad didn't want us to get into trouble. Remember? He told us to stay together."

"Going to the library isn't trouble. And you're coming with me."

I tilted my head at Drew, wrinkled my eyebrows, and gave him a pleading look. Surely Drew wouldn't allow this.

I was wrong.

"Come on, boy. Looks like we're going to the library."
He sighed and rubbed my ears. I licked his hand mournfully.

Drew grumbled, though not quietly. "The only reason
we're going, Hopscotch, is because Dad told us to stay
together." After we got on his bike, he pedaled fast to catch
up to Camilla, who had pulled over on the side of the road.

Lines of people stood on the sidewalk on their
tiptoes, as if there were a parade.

"What's going on?" Drew asked when we caught up.

Camilla shook her head. "I don't know yet."

We found out pretty quickly.

Police cars lined the street in front of our favorite gas
station. Several police officers bustled about—some with
notebooks, some with cameras. The whole area was taped
off.

"What do you think happened?" Camilla asked.

"I don't know. You think that's the new case Dad's
working on?"

"Must be. Not much happens in this town."

We watched them work for a while, the policemen questioning the gas station owner and pointing to the camera on the front of the store, before Camilla said, "Come on. The policemen need space to work."

When we got to the library, Drew graciously helped me off his bike before letting the bike flop haphazardly on the ground. "Let's get this over with," he groaned.

"Hold on. I'm just going to lock up our bikes," Camilla replied. She fidgeted with her bike and lock, then picked up Drew's bike and locked it up as well.

Drew raised his eyebrows. "You seriously think someone in this town is going to steal our bikes?"

"Better safe than sorry," Camilla said. "Besides, we did just see some sort of investigation down the street."

I vividly remembered the last time we came to the library. The tennis ball bouncing off my nose, straight through the window . . . It wasn't good.

When we walked in, Mrs. Johnson smiled and waved when she saw Camilla. Her hair was pulled into a tight bun, and her skirt and blouse screamed of order. Her eyebrows furrowed when she saw Drew, and her smile wavered just a little. Then her eyes landed on me. She obviously hadn't forgotten about the window either.

"I'm sorry, Camilla, but dogs are not allowed inside. He'll have to wait outside."

"But, Mrs. Johnson, he's a really good dog. We're training him to become a support dog."

"A support dog?" I could practically see the wheels turning in Mrs. Johnson's head.

"Yes," Camilla answered. "A support dog."

Drew bent over and whispered into my ear, "I've never heard her tell a lie. Ever. She's always such a goody-two-shoes!"

"You see," Camilla lowered her voice, leaning in close to the older lady. In the library light, the splatter of freckles danced across the girl's cheeks. "Drew needs emotional support. Daddy says that he's very impulsive and unstable, and having Hopscotch with him helps him stay calm. It's much better to have them together. Promise." She drew a cross over her heart.

Drew's mouth hung open. "I—"

I knew what he was going to say. He was going to deny every word Camilla had just said, and it would ruin Camilla's plan. I stepped on Drew's foot and nudged his hand with my nose.

When Mrs. Johnson looked over at us, she saw Drew's hand resting on top of my head, like the best friends we were. The librarian shook her head but said, "Next time, he needs a vest to come inside. A vest that says he's a support dog."

"Yes, ma'am," Camilla said. "Thank you." She waited for just a moment. "Mrs. Johnson, if I found a library card, would you be able to tell me whose it was?"

"No," Mrs. Johnson answered, typing away at her computer now. "We have to keep things really confidential over here. But if you found a card, I'll gladly hold on to it until they come in looking for it."

"Oh, no, it was just a question," Camilla replied, flipping her hair. "You know how Drew is always losing things."

10

"I see," she said. "Well, let me know if you need any help."

"We will. Thank you." Camilla turned to us. "Come on. We need to use a computer."

We followed her to a row of bright screens.

"I need 'emotional support'?" Drew hissed. "And I'm always losing things? That's not funny."

Camilla giggled. "I thought it was. Besides, the first lie got both of you inside the library, and the second one wasn't even a lie."

All the computers were being used except for one. She headed right for it.

"So, how is the computer going to help us return the wallet?" Drew whispered.

"We're going to hack the computer system."

I snapped my head to Camilla. This was a whole new side of her.

"Since when do you know how to hack?" Drew asked.

"Since just now. It can't be that hard. I'll figure it out."

Drew folded his arms and narrowed his eyes. "Hacking isn't something you learn in a day. I'll do the hacking." Racing to the computer, he grabbed the chair at the same time Camilla did. He tried to clamber in, but Camilla booted him out of the seat. He stumbled backward, directly into a teenager leaving the next computer. Drew and the teenager sprawled onto the floor.

"Get off me," the teenager said, shoving Drew. Drew hopped up and held out his hand to help the teenager up. The stranger grabbed Drew's hand. His pointer finger, black and blue, was swollen and missing a fingernail. The odor of dirt, gravel, BO, and concrete almost overwhelmed my sensitive nose.

Drew brushed himself off. "That's a nasty bruise on your finger. What happened?"

"Oh, it's nothing." The teenager rubbed his hands together. "I work in construction. I hammered my finger instead of the nail."

I approached the older kid and sniffed him closer. There was something enticing about a smell that strong. Like he hadn't showered in a week.

He tensed as I sniffed his leg. "I've got to go. Bye."

We watched him skirt between the rows of books and dash out the door.

"Man, he was awkward," Drew whispered. "Remind me never to become a teenager."

"So awkward. Maybe he just doesn't like dogs."

I plopped down by the chair and scratched my ear. Who wouldn't like dogs? We're man's best friend. I groaned as I caught the itch, then stretched into a comfortable position, on my back with my three paws sprawled out in the air.

Camilla watched me for a second before shaking her head. I didn't think my position looked funny. It was comfortable.

Sitting in front of the computer she clicked a lot and pulled up a blue screen, but then it went back to the normal screen.

After several minutes, Drew interrupted. "You don't know what you're doing, do you?"

"I do too." *Click, click, click.*

This lie wasn't nearly as convincing as her last one.

"Here, scoot over." Drew pulled on her chair.

Camilla surrendered the chair, but she watched her twin closely. "Where did you learn how to hack?"

With a shrug of his shoulders, he said innocently, "I learned it at school."

"You . . . learned how to hack at school?"

"Don't worry about it." Drew stared at the screen intently, although he wasn't doing much either.

"You did get surprisingly good grades this year. Dad was really proud of you. Remember, he took you to Krispy Kreme and you got a donut for each A?"

Drew clenched his jaw, and his face got all splotchy and red. He wiped his hands on his jeans. Sweat. I licked his jeans.

Camilla's eyes widened. "Is that how you learned to hack? By changing your grades?"

14

Drew's silence was answer enough.

"Oh my gosh. My brother is a cheater. *My twin brother is a cheater.* Oh my gosh. I have to tell Dad. I have to—"

"Don't you dare!" Drew exclaimed. A few people in the library shushed him. Lowering his voice, he said, "Look. Dad was really proud of me, and I did *try* to get good grades. They just weren't as good as yours. Please. Dad would kill me. I just wanted to make him proud of me, like he is of you." He rubbed his hands on his cheeks. "I won't do it again. I promise."

Camilla stared at him and chewed her lip, a sign that she was thinking. "Fine," she said. She held out her pinky, and Drew took it, sealing the promise. "Never again."

"Now," Drew cracked his fingers like a pianist about to begin his masterpiece, "let's get to work."

## Chapter 3

Drew began typing, his fingers flying across the keyboard. The bright blue background on the computer shifted to black, with lines of white and yellow letters and numbers that made no sense to Camilla or me. Human language is difficult to read, even if it's not difficult to understand. After another minute of typing, Drew smiled proudly. "There! A list of all the library card numbers and their owners."

"I can't believe I'm saying this, but nice work, Drew," Camilla murmured.

Drew did a quick search for the library card number. "Here it is." He pointed to the screen. "Hayes. It says his address is 565 Center Street."

"Hayes?" Camilla asked, squinting at the screen. "Like, Matt Hayes from school?" I noticed a slight blush creeping onto her cheeks and a small tremor in her voice.

"It could be," Drew shrugged.

Camilla fidgeted with her shorts and tucked her hair behind her ears. "Right, okay. I . . . I guess we'll take it over there." She smoothed her hair down. "Let's go."

"Why are you acting all funny?" Drew asked as he watched her.

"I'm not," she argued. "Come on, let's go."

"You don't like him, do you? He's a jock!"

"Matt is also extremely smart." She turned and stalked out of the library, but she didn't deny his claim.

"Wow, she's sensitive," Drew muttered.

I rested my head on Drew's leg to show my sympathy. He was a little rude to her, but I wasn't going to be the one to tell him.

"Come on, boy. I guess we'd better follow her."

Mrs. Johnson eyed Drew and me as we exited the library. As the door swung shut, I heard an almost inaudible sigh of relief.

House 565 was not special or unusual in any way. It sat between other unremarkable houses, each just as dull and unnoticeable.

Leaving his bike toppled on the sidewalk—much to Camilla's dismay—Drew walked up to the house and knocked. Camilla and I met him on the doorstep. After a minute, a girl just younger than the twins answered the door. She had deep blue eyes and blonde-streaked light brown hair. Before she could say anything, a boy appeared behind her, with the same blue eyes and light brown hair. A purple bruise colored the corner of his forehead. He froze when he saw Camilla, then glanced up and down the street.

"They're here for me, Madelyn," the boy said. His hands shook as he grabbed the door. "Thanks."

She shrugged and walked off. The noise from the TV echoed throughout the house. The boy continued to look up and down the street.

"Matt, are you okay?" Camilla asked, watching him. "What are you looking for?"

"I'm fine. What are you doing here? When did you get a dog? Come in. Don't just stand out there. Hurry up."

Drew shot Camilla a bewildered look before he stepped inside. Camilla and I shimmied through the small gap in the door behind him.

"Matt, meet Hopscotch," Drew said when the door closed behind us.

"Not here," Matt whispered. "Follow me."

We followed him through the kitchen and down the hallway to his bedroom. Minecraft posters plastered the walls, and a small basketball hoop hung from the corner window. His dark-blue blanket was rumpled on the bed. Pictures of himself and Madelyn dotted the walls and his dresser, but I noticed there were none of his parents. He slammed the door behind us. A line of seven locks trailed down the door.

Matt locked all seven locks on the door, nodding and murmuring. Finally, he sighed and plopped down on the bed.

"You were saying?" he prodded Drew.

"This is Hopscotch. We adopted him at the beginning of the summer."

Matt looked down at me. "You named a three-legged dog *Hopscotch*?"

Drew grinned broadly. "That was my idea. Because he has a little hop when he walks."

"What happened to his leg?" Matt asked.

Drew shrugged. "We don't know. The Humane Shelter found him that way."

My heart tugged a little in my chest as I thought of Mikey, the four-year-old boy I had to leave behind. I shook my head and brought myself back to the present moment.

Camilla held out her hand shyly, the wallet in her palm. "We found this at the park. We thought it might be yours."

He grabbed it and turned it over. He checked inside. "Thanks! I've been missing this." He pulled out a ten-dollar bill. "And thanks for not taking my money."

"Camilla wouldn't let me," Drew joked. Camilla elbowed him in the side.

"How did you know it was mine?"

A wicked smile lit up Drew's face as he rubbed his ribs. "We hacked into the library system to find out who the library card belonged to. It was Camilla's idea, but I did the hacking."

Camilla elbowed him again.

"Ouch," Drew growled, rubbing his side. "Stop that."

21

"Seriously?" Matt blinked. "You guys, that is totally awesome!"

Drew beamed, but Camilla turned bright red.

A horn honked from across the street. Matt froze and held up a hand. "Wait." He inched to the window, pulled back the drapes, and watched as a black sedan pulled out of his neighbor's driveway.

Camilla whispered, "Matt, are you okay? What's going on?"

Matt waited until the car was out of sight. "I'm fine. I'm just . . . just . . . I'm okay."

"What's going on?" she asked. "What's up with all the locks?"

Matt gulped nervously. "Oh, you noticed? I was trying to play it cool."

"It's not working," Drew said.

Matt licked his lips nervously. "I think I'm being followed."

"Why would someone be following you?" Camilla asked.

"I don't know. It's just this red truck I keep seeing. It follows me to swim practice, or when I go to a friend's house. It drives past my house at least once a day."

"Do you know who it is?" Drew asked.

"No." Matt started to breathe faster. He was starting to panic. I sat next to him and nudged his hand with my nose. He knelt down and petted me. Soon enough, his breathing calmed down a little.

He took a deep breath and continued his story. "There . . . there was an incident, a couple of days ago. I can't give you all the details, but I—I think I saw something, something I wasn't supposed to. But I can't remember what it was." His eyes, unfocused and hazy, stared at something far away from us.

"Okay, man, you're creeping me out." Drew slid closer to the door, placing his hand on the doorknob.

"Wait—wait." Matt placed his hand on Drew's arm. "Did you guys find my wallet by yourselves?"

"We used a computer, but other than that, yeah," Drew responded.

"Would you be able to do it again?" Matt wiped the sweat from his forehead.

"Do what again?"

Matt held his wallet back out to the twins. "I have ten dollars," he said. "It's all I have. But I want to hire you."

"Hire us to do what, exactly?" Camilla asked.

Matt swallowed. "I need your help finding something. Something I lost."

"What did you lose?" Camilla asked.

"My memories."

# Chapter 4

I tilted my head. Was he serious? The twins stared at the nervous boy.

Matt looked from Drew to Camilla, then hurried to explain. "I really don't remember much from the incident. I blacked out and woke up on the sidewalk. My head hurt like the devil, and my bike was gone."

Camilla poked Drew's arm. "You see?" she said. "People in this town *do* steal bikes."

Drew narrowed his eyes at her, but Matt ignored their argument. "Please. Some truck has been following me and I'm scared. If I remember what I've forgotten, maybe I can get the person to leave me alone."

"Yes, you've mentioned the truck," Drew said, nodding. He placed his finger on his chin. "We might be able to get to the bottom of this."

Camilla pulled on Drew's arm, dragging him to the corner of the room. "Just one second, Matt," she said with a smile. Then she turned and whispered to Drew. "I don't think we should get involved."

I stood next to her and rubbed my head against her leg. I agreed wholeheartedly. I still hadn't had my afternoon nap yet.

"What about the money?" Drew murmured. "We could buy ten candy bars with that!"

"Dad told us to stay out of trouble. He'll be so mad if he figures out what we're doing. He always tells us to leave things to the police, to let them do the work. Plus, he's working some new case and—"

Matt interrupted her. He apparently could hear every word they were saying. "That's why I can't go to the police. I know they're busy catching real criminals." He paused for a second before continuing. "Please. If something happened to Madelyn or to my mom because of me . . ."

He was close to tears, I knew. I licked his fingers. He smooshed my cheeks together and kissed my forehead.

"Has the truck actually stopped to talk to you or anyone in your family?" Camilla asked.

Matt shook his head.

"How much time is missing? From your memories?" Drew asked.

"A couple of hours. I was going to meet up with Spencer at his house, but I don't think I ever made it there."

We took in the information, then Camilla said, "Listen, Matt, it's not like your memories are going to be in a lost-and-found box. This job you're hiring us for will be nearly impossible."

"I know, I know. Memories aren't tangible. But I need to know what happened to me, and I want this truck gone. And I want my bike back too. Please, Camilla—you're the only one I can count on."

27

The color of her cheeks matched her hair, yet she seemed pleased. She met Drew's eyes.

There's something about twins where they can share a look and have an entire conversation that only they are privy to. I watched Drew and Camilla communicate silently in that way. When they made their decision, I sighed. My lazy lifestyle was about to change.

Drew stuck out his hand. "We'll help you."

Matt, gratefully, shook his hand. "Okay, great. Where do we start?"

Drew and Matt stared at each other. Camilla sighed and held out her hand. "Hand me your phone, Matt."

He dug into his pockets and pulled out a little black cell phone.

Camilla typed in a number and held the phone to her ear. I listened to the ring of the phone on the other end.

"What is she doing?" Matt whispered.

"She's calling the police station. Dad makes us practice it so much that I bet even Hopscotch could dial it."

Matt looked like he was going to say something, but his answer was cut off.

"Hello, Officer Downs. I've lost my bike. Has anyone called it in, perhaps? Yes, of course I'll wait."

"First she lied to the librarian, now she's lying to Officer Downs." Drew shook his head, but a small smile curved his mouth. "I'm so proud."

The music ringing from the phone speaker was soft, light. Elevator music. Matt's and Drew's ears weren't sensitive enough to hear it, but it was making me sleepy. I yawned and snuggled myself into a little ball.

The music stopped and Officer Downs spoke again.

"Okay, thank you," Camilla said. She hung up the phone. "No one has reported a lost bike or a found bike. So whoever found your bike wasn't trying to be a Good Samaritan. He or she definitely stole it."

The grandfather clock in Matt's house announced the time. Five dings.

Drew and Camilla looked at Matt's alarm clock. "It's five o'clock! Dad's going to be home soon. We've got to go!"

Drew scurried to the door, his fingers fumbling to unlock all the bolts on the door. "Come by tomorrow morning. We'll start working on it then. Bye!"

We raced home, me running next to them to save time, and burst through the door seconds before Mr. Walker's car pulled around the corner and the garage door opened.

I was hot. My tongue hung out of my mouth as I crawled to the water bowl and lapped up every drop of water I could.

Mr. Walker barged through the door and swung the twins around in a big hug. "What are you feeling for dinner tonight? Pizza?"

The twins responded with an emphatic, "Yes!"

During dinner, Mr. Walker asked the twins what they had done that day. They answered briefly, not meeting his eyes. He looked down at me. Suspicion clouded his eyes. I buried my eyes behind my paws.

My job was to keep them out of trouble, yet they had taken a job with trouble spelled all over it.

# Chapter 5

A high-pitched buzzing woke me up. Mr. Walker's cell phone. I yawned, blinked, and stretched. The black windows told me that it was still the middle of the night. It wasn't the first time his phone had gone off in the middle of the night, nor would it likely be the last.

"Detective Walker." His whisper floated down the stairs to my bed in the kitchen. I didn't normally sleep with the twins, despite their begging. It reminded me too much of my past life, my past family. Sometimes, though, it was needed. Tonight would be one of those nights.

"I see. I'll be right there."

After a few minutes, his feet thumped down the stairs. His keys jingled in his pockets.

"Hey, Hopscotch," he said when he saw me watching. "Some teenagers are making too much noise for Mrs. Adley. You take care of them, okay?"

He didn't have to tell me who "them" was. I let out a quiet, affirmative yowl.

It seemed that every day that Mr. Walker was on call, there was a party that Mrs. Adley thought was too loud; usually, though, it was a group of friends roasting marshmallows in someone's backyard, or projecting a movie onto the side of the house. Brookhaven, and Mrs. Adley, took noise-level enforcement very seriously.

"Good boy. I'll be back soon."

He closed the garage door behind him, and I trotted upstairs into Drew and Camilla's room. Camilla's bed was closer to the door, so I hopped up next to her. Besides, Drew slept with his mouth open, and more often than not, there was a puddle of drool on his pillow. Careful not to crinkle the picture of her mother she kept under her pillow, I snuggled close to the girl.

"Hey, Hoppy," she murmured, then fell back asleep. Within seconds, I fell back asleep, too.

Sometime later, Mr. Walker crept into the room and pressed a kiss on each of our foreheads, including mine. He certainly loved his kids, and maybe he loved me, then, too.

A minute later, I heard his snores.

***

It wasn't long after I scarfed down the last piece of bacon that the doorbell rang.

Drew was at the kitchen table, mopping up his syrup with his pancake. His hair stood up in all directions.

"Coming!" Camilla shouted.

I raced her to the front door, my tail wagging excitedly. Camilla peered through the peephole, smoothed down her clothes, then threw the door open. Matt stood there in a baseball cap and sunglasses.

"Can I come in?" he asked. He shifted from one foot to the other nervously. "Please?"

Camilla stood back and let him in.

"Thanks."

Matt went directly to the windows and started closing the blinds.

"You're still scared, huh?" Camilla asked, watching him.

"No," Matt answered. "Nervous. I'm nervous and cautious. Can't take any risks."

Drew waved when he saw Matt in the family room. "Hey, Matt," he said. A glob of brown syrup dribbled down his chin. "I'll be ready in a minute."

Matt took off his sunglasses and hat and examined some of the pictures hanging on the wall. Some were of the twins, one of their mother, and one as a whole family before the "incident." That's what Drew calls his mother's death, anyway—the "incident."

"You have your mother's eyes," Matt said, examining the family picture.

A shy smile toyed on Camilla's lips. "That's what everyone says."

"I'm sorry about what happened."

Camilla looked down at the floor. "Thanks," she finally said, her voice wobbly. "It's been a rough year." I sauntered over and licked her fingers. She scratched my nose in return.

Matt moved his hand, hovered it above her shoulder, but then returned it to his side. "If you ever want someone to talk to, I'm here. When my dad died, I felt so alone. And no one knew what to say."

"Thanks," she said. "I appreciate that." She hesitated for just a moment more before continuing. "And I may take you up on that. Drew . . . well, he doesn't like to talk about it."

Matt slowly placed his hand on Camilla's shoulder. My ears, more sensitive than a human's, listened to Camilla's heart racing. Her eyes met his and they both smiled.

Drew's crashing footsteps on the stairs startled all of us, ruining the moment. Matt whisked his hand away. Camilla knelt on the ground and rubbed my ears. I didn't complain.

"You ready to get started?" Drew asked, oblivious to the scene he was interrupting.

"Yes," Matt said. "How do we start?"

Drew held up a long loop of cloth. It was Mr. Walker's spare lanyard, where he usually kept his keys. "You," Drew said dramatically, "need to remember." He beckoned Matt toward the sofa. I took the empty seat next to Matt, hoping for a few extra pets.

"Get down, Hopscotch. Matt needs to lie down," Drew said. "It'll be easier to put him into a trance."

"A trance?" Matt and Camilla said at the same time.

"Yes, a trance. We're going to unlock Matt's memories. They're there; we just have to access them."

"And how," Camilla asked, "are you going to do that?"

"Hypnosis, of course."

I choked in an attempt to laugh. A few days earlier, we had watched a scary movie about a man who couldn't remember who he was. He went to a psychiatrist, who hypnotized him, but the psychiatrist ended up being the bad guy. The good news is that the hypnosis worked, because it released memories and clues that the main character needed to solve the mystery. That was a movie, though, and this was real life.

Camilla stared at her brother. The surprise written on her face was well hidden, but it was still there. She grabbed his arm and turned him around. She muttered just loud enough for me to hear, but not Matt.

"Maybe we should try something more conventional," she said. "Hypnosis is—well, let's go see Spencer first. Spencer saw him last. He might know what happened."

"Or maybe," Drew interrupted, his eyes widening, and he turned to Matt. "Maybe it was Spencer who took your bike."

"Why would Spencer do that? He's my best friend."

"I don't know, but he's the last person to see you before you lost your bike, which makes him a suspect. Come on. Let's go."

Spencer's house wasn't far away. Since Matt's bike was lost, Drew offered him my spot on the back of his bike.

Matt spread out my blanket on the metal cage, complaining of the smell. I grumbled, plotting ways to get back at him while I trotted resignedly to Spencer's house.

We hadn't gone far before Drew and Camilla slammed on their brakes, screeching to a halt. I caught up to them, watching them curiously.

"Shhh," Drew warned us.

I poked my head around Drew and Matt. I saw a boy with a fat face and messy brown hair drooping over his forehead. He wasn't paying any attention to us. He was focused on a young kid, who had tears streaming down his face.

"You wanna say that again, punk?" the fat boy said.

The young boy shook his head.

"It's Ryan Lewis," Camilla whispered. "The biggest bully from school. We don't want him to see us."

I agreed. He looked like trouble.

"I didn't think so!" Ryan shouted at the kid. "Now, go home. Before I give you a *good* reason to cry."

The kid ran, wiping snot into his dirtied sleeve. Then Ryan turned and saw us.

"Go. Go, go go!" Drew shouted.

He and Camilla turned their bikes around and pedaled as fast as they could. Rocks flew past us, landing on the sidewalk. A glance over my shoulder confirmed my suspicions: Ryan was throwing rocks at us. A pebble flew past and hit Drew in the back of the head. He yelped and put his hand to his head, but he didn't stop.

When we were out of range, Matt covered his head with my blanket, even though he had donned his baseball cap and sunglasses. His own mother wouldn't recognize him. I sure hoped Spencer had useful information, because Matt's disguises were getting ridiculous.

But the blond-haired boy didn't have any news for us.

"Matt and I were *supposed* to play games," Spencer said when he met us at the door, "but he never showed. I called your house, Matt, and your mom said you'd already left, but you never showed up. And what happened to your forehead?"

Matt fingered the bruise above his eye. "It's a long story," he answered.

A little girl in a glittery ballerina tutu appeared behind Spencer and shrieked. "Is that a puppy? Can I pet him?"

Glitter fell to the floor like rain in a storm. I grimaced inwardly. Glitter on my coat wouldn't come out easily, if at all. I shuddered to think of the pink sparkles that would be embedded in my skin forever. But I gave my best impression of a smile and trotted inside to meet the girl.

"This is Spencer's sister, Tiffany," Matt introduced.

"Today's my birthday, and I'm four!" Tiffany announced.

Her hands were soft as she pet me. She wasn't much older than Mikey, and the realization made me miss the little boy even more. His blond hair and blue eyes danced before my eyes as I remembered him trying to use his lasso on me. He never did quite get the hang of it, and I never stood still long enough for him to get good at it.

Tiffany, unaware of my wandering thoughts, rubbed my cheeks, smooshing them together and bringing my face forward to meet hers. I pushed the memories of Mikey away and licked her nose. She giggled and ran away. Her nose tasted like frosting. I licked my lips, getting a hint of the strawberry flavor in my mouth again. Yum.

A minute later, she appeared again, this time with a ball. I eyed the ball and pranced over to her. "Come on, doggie," she said, walking out the front door. "Let's play fetch."

I followed her into the front yard, my tail wagging incessantly. Nothing was better than a good game of fetch. Swinging her arm around and around, she finally let go. The ball bounced about four inches in front of me, but I didn't mind. I jumped over to it, picked it up with my mouth, and brought it back to her. Once more, the ball was in her hand. I stared at it, waiting for it to move. But Tiffany wasn't moving her arm. She was looking at something.

I followed her gaze. A rusted red pickup truck rambled along slowly, much slower than needed. The driver waved a BB gun out the open window. Tiffany screamed.

41

## Chapter 6

Spencer swung the door open. "Tiffany! Get in here!"

Tiffany, still in her ballerina costume, did not need to be told twice. She and I took off and plowed through the door together.

Spencer pulled his sister into him, then looked at the four of us. "What's going on here, guys?"

Color crept onto Matt's neck. "It's my fault, Spencer. I'm sorry. I didn't think they'd follow me here. Someone's looking for me. Or keeping an eye on me. I think they're making sure I don't talk."

"Who? Talk about what?" Spencer pressed.

Matt shook his head. "I don't know. I don't remember. I was hoping you could tell me. Tell me what happened that day."

"I told you already," Spencer said. "You never showed up. It was about seven o'clock when I called your house. There's nothing more to tell."

"Did you see anything? Hear anything?" Camilla jumped in for the first time. "Anything you remember could be important."

"No, nothing." Spencer shook his head. He paused, then said, "Well, maybe one thing."

We waited patiently.

"You know Ryan?"

Drew scowled as he rubbed the back of his head. I'm sure he was still remembering the rock that Ryan had just thrown at him. "Of course we know Ryan. He's on my baseball team, and he makes baseball suck."

"Well, I saw him sneaking through the bushes in the backyard, heading to the baseball diamond. Coach Jackson was there with the second-grade team."

"Maybe Ryan was there to help coach," Camilla suggested.

43

Drew scoffed. "Ryan doesn't help anyone do anything."

"If he was supposed to be there, then why would he be sneaking?" Spencer asked. "He kept looking over his shoulder, then darted through the bushes and across the street. He was nervous."

"Even if he was doing something bad, how do you know it's related to Matt?" Camilla objected. "Baseball doesn't have anything to do with our case."

"Maybe it does," Drew said. "We don't know what happened to Matt that night, or where he went. Maybe he rode down by the baseball diamond and Ryan saw him. Maybe it was a baseball bat that hit Matt. It doesn't hurt to look into it."

"I agree with Drew," Matt interrupted. "Anything involving Ryan is bad news."

"He's not old enough to drive, though," Camilla pointed out. "That can't be him that just drove past in the truck."

"Maybe he has some older friends, or an older brother. I don't care. We've got to find out what he was up to. Especially if it has to do with those kids," Drew said.

"Good luck," Spencer said. "I wish I could come with you guys. It's Tiffany's birthday party tonight." He winced, as if the thought of a ballerina birthday party caused him actual pain. For all I know, it could have.

After saying goodbye, Drew and Matt decided to go check out Ryan right then. Camilla groaned but followed the boys to the bikes. Matt pulled a bandana out of his pocket and tied it around his head. He looked ridiculous.

"This way. Slowly." Matt pointed to the right. "He lives just down here. Here's what we're going to do."

As he whispered the plan to Drew and Camilla, I let out a small whimper. I didn't like this plan.

Minutes later, Camilla and I took our place at Ryan's front door. She rang the doorbell, then turned and gave Matt and Drew a thumbs-up. A loud racket inside startled us. It sounded like a birdcage falling down the stairs.

45

"I hope you know what you're doing, Matt," Camilla grumbled.

I hoped so, too.

"What are you doing here, Carrot Head?" sneered the boy who opened the door. Up close, I could tell that he was tall for his age and had several extra layers of fat.

"I lost my dog's ball. I think it bounced into your backyard." Camilla let the lie slip from her lips, but she couldn't disguise her disgust of either Ryan or the lie.

"If your ball was in my backyard, then it's not your ball anymore. Get out of here." He moved to close the door, but she wedged in her foot before it slammed shut.

"It's his favorite ball," she said. "He's not the same without it."

"I haven't seen it."

While Camilla spoke with the bully, Matt and Drew darted off to the side of the house, dirt smudged on their faces for camouflage. Camilla had tried to tell them that it didn't help, but Drew wanted to look to play the part of "undercover" correctly.

Camilla kept Ryan's attention while the boys snuck through the door on the side of the house and into the garage. They'd have to hurry.

"Maybe I can go look," Camilla offered.

"Maybe you can leave," he taunted. "You're not going into my yard."

"Ry-Ry, who are you talking to?" A young girl, no older than six, peeked out from behind Ryan's wide figure. "Wow, she's pretty, Ry. Is she your girlfriend? What's her name?"

Camilla blinked, but then bent down and extended her hand to the girl for a handshake. "Camilla. Camilla Walker. I go to school with Ryan."

"I like school. I'm going into first grade soon! Aren't you going to let her come in, Ryan?" She tugged on his shirt. "You should invite your girlfriend inside. She's nice."

Camilla's face flushed as she took a step back.

"No, Jessica, she's not my girlfriend. And she has to go anyway, right, Camilla?"

"Actually," Camilla said to Jessica before the door could close, "I think I accidentally threw my dog's ball in your backyard. Could you go look for it for me?"

"Sure!" The wave of brown hair bounced as she skipped down the hallway.

"She's cute," Camilla said. "She's your sister?"

"Stepsister," Ryan grunted. "Where's Drew?"

Camilla swallowed. "He's not feeling well. He's at home."

Ryan narrowed his eyes and folded his arms. "I hit him with a rock just a little while ago."

48

"Yes, and now he has a headache. He went home."

I had to admit, Camilla was a pretty good liar.

"I didn't even know you had a dog."

"We got him at the beginning of the summer."

"Stop fooling around. What are you really doing here? I bet that dog doesn't have a ball. He doesn't even have a collar."

"I . . . I . . ."

A loud crash echoed throughout the house. It sounded like it came from the garage. Uh oh.

"What was that?" Ryan turned. His face burned red in anger. "Is Drew in the garage? I'm going to kill—"

Jessica returned. "I didn't see anything in the backyard. I hope Scampers isn't getting into things again. Daddy wasn't happy last time." Her eyes studied her purple toenails.

"Thanks for checking, Jessica." Camilla smiled.

Another crash sounded.

Ryan glared at Camilla. "Excuse me," he snarled. "I'll go check on that cat."

49

I did what any dog would do. I began to howl. I howled and yowled and barked as loud as I could.

"Shut up! Shut him up! Why is he barking?"

"Um . . . cats," Camilla answered. "He doesn't like cats. We've got to go. Nice to meet you, Jessica!"

Camilla dashed across the yard with me on her heels. Matt and Drew scrambled out of the garage and chased us down the street. Ryan, still in the doorway, yelled and screamed, but he didn't follow us.

We didn't stop until we reached our bikes.

Drew collapsed onto the ground, but Camilla and Matt leaned against the fence to catch their breaths. Matt held a hand to his side as if to ease a cramp.

"Did you find anything?" Camilla asked between pants.

"If he stole Matt's bike, it wasn't in the garage," Drew said.

"Where else would he have put it?" Matt wondered. He was fully recovered now and pacing the sidewalk.

"Maybe he didn't take it," Camilla muttered. Everyone ignored her.

"Let's follow him and see what happens. Wherever he goes, we go."

Camilla raised an eyebrow. "Oh? And how are we going to do that?"

Drew smiled. "I have just the idea."

## Chapter 7

Camilla looked at the device Drew placed in her hand. We were back at our place, and Drew had just climbed down from the attic. There was so much dust up there. I'd never sneezed so much in my life. "A walkie-talkie? Are you serious?"

"This is seriously outdated, Drew," Matt said, pulling at a frayed wire.

"It's ingenious!" Drew said. "We'll split the day into three parts. Morning, afternoon, and evening."

I sniffed the so-called walkie-talkies. They smelled like dust. They probably hadn't been out of the attic since the twins were in kindergarten. Or before.

"I get up earlier, so I'll take mornings," Camilla volunteered, though she didn't seem happy about her assignment. "How long is this going to last?"

Drew ignored her question. "I'll take evenings. That's when Ryan and I have baseball practice anyway, so that'll be best." He nodded to himself. He looked proud of his plan.

"What exactly are we looking for?" Matt asked as he flipped the walkie-talkie over.

"Anything suspicious. If he meets with anyone, steals anything—"

"Or drives a red truck," Camilla inserted.

"Exactly."

"When do we start?" Matt asked.

Drew looked down at his watch. My stomach rumbled on cue. I knew what time it was. Lunchtime.

"Let's start after lunch," Drew said. "We just saw him at his house, so he won't go too far, I don't think. We'll regroup when we have more info."

Matt took that as his cue to leave. "Let me know if you come up with anything." He looked directly at Camilla. "Bye, Cam."

"Bye," she whispered, her fingers waving slightly as he whisked past.

Drew shook his head. "You're pathetic. He's still wearing that awful cap and his sunglasses! How can you be attracted to that? And when did you start going by Cam?"

Camilla didn't answer. She walked into the kitchen and started preparing sandwiches. I sat next to her feet, hoping for an extra little snack.

She didn't disappoint me. A small piece of ham fell on the counter, and she flicked it off the counter and into my mouth.

Drew eventually followed and plopped himself onto a chair. "Are you packing a lunch for Dad?" he asked.

"Yep. I thought he might like a visit."

Camilla folded the sandwiches into a Tupperware and added a few cookies inside. A drop of saliva slipped off my tongue and fell onto the floor.

When we got to the police station, Mr. Walker didn't notice our arrival. We snuck over to his desk to wait for him. As we made our way through the room, a plate of unattended donuts caught my eye. I crept over, stuck my head over the desk, and snatched one before anyone noticed. A few sprinkles fell unnoticed to the floor.

The place was a mess. Normally, the station was quiet. Not much goes on in the small town of Brookhaven. But today, something had the office in an uproar. Phones rang continuously, papers flew through the air, and the maze of desks was pushed off to the side of the room to make way for a whiteboard filled with pictures and human writing.

Mr. Walker conversed quietly and hurriedly to another police officer. She was tall and slim, with jet-black hair cascading down her back. He smiled when she said something, and she touched his arm. When he saw us, he said something else to her, then picked his way through the catastrophe toward us. Spotting the Tupperware, he said, "Let's go in the conference room. There's more space there."

Camilla and Drew sat at the large table, in chairs with wheels that spun around in circles. I took my spot behind them, on my green-and-brown woven rug. It really was an ugly rug, but it was more comfortable than the hardwood floor in the conference room. Mr. Walker bought it at a yard sale specifically for when I came to visit.

"What brings you two in?" Mr. Walker asked as he stuffed a piece of sandwich in his mouth.

I lifted my head and whined.

"Sorry, boy. What brings you *three* in today?"

I settled my head back down on my paws contentedly.

"Who was that officer?" Camilla questioned.

"That," Mr. Walker said, "is Detective Arianna Mills. She just transferred here, and she's my new partner."

Camilla and Drew looked at each other, their unspoken conversation speaking volumes. I wasn't the only one who picked up on it.

"Don't worry," Mr. Walker said. "There's nothing like that between us. You wanna tell me why you're here?"

"Well . . ." Camilla started. She explained everything—well, nearly everything—from the lost wallet, to finding Matt, to Matt hiring them to help find his bike. She skipped over the parts about Matt missing his memories and the big bruise on his forehead.

"He should have come to the police," Mr. Walker stated firmly.

"He didn't want to bother you. It looks like you're super busy." Drew grabbed a cookie, but Camilla smacked his hand.

"We are. I'll tell you as much as I can. You know that gas station you two love so much? Well, it was robbed."

"Robbed?" Camilla gasped. "Like, *robbed* robbed? We saw a whole lot of police offers and police cars, but we didn't know what happened."

"Several hundred dollars are missing from the cash register, the place is trashed, and poor Frank, the owner, is scared out of his wits," Mr. Walker explained.

"Did anyone see the robber?" Drew asked.

"Frank did. But the robber was wearing a ski mask. Couldn't make out any features. The robber had a gun. All Frank could do was stare at the barrel of the gun."

"Poor Frank!"

Mr. Walker nodded grimly. "We aren't telling the press about it. We don't want to scare our thief. We don't want to scare him out of town, and we think he's a local. No one else really comes to Brookhaven; it's too small of a town."

"Why would someone rob Frank?" Camilla wondered. "He's just a harmless old man."

"Who gives out free slushies," Drew added.

"We're still trying to figure it out. Now," Mr. Walker said sternly, "don't tell anyone about this. A few rumors are going around, but I don't want you to go around confirming or denying those. No information can get to our robber. Deal?"

"Deal," the twins answered.

Mr. Walker wasn't done yet, though. "And I don't want you to go near Frank. He's a mess, and there's a chance the robber will come back. Understand?"

They mumbled a "yes sir," then chewed in silence for a few minutes before Drew threw the crusts of his sandwich to me. "Dad," he said thoughtfully, "when you have a suspect, what's your next step?"

"What do *I* do, or what do *you* do?" Mr. Walker replied suspiciously. "There's a difference. There needs to be a reason—a motive—for why your suspect would commit the crime. Then you need to have proof that they're the one who did it. When *I* have those things, I arrest the suspect. But you two aren't the police. If you have any evidence of what happened, you come to the police. Okay?"

The twins exchanged another look. "Okay," replied Drew. "If we find proof, we'll come to you."

Mr. Walker seemed satisfied with that answer. "Thanks for lunch. I have get back to work now. I'll be home late tonight, so don't wait up. And you know where to reach me if you need me."

"Yep. Bye, Dad," they said in unison.

As we left the station, Drew said, "I've got baseball practice in a few. I'm going to go early and warm up." He hopped on his bike, then turned back to Camilla. "Do you think Dad will get us cell phones for our birthday?"

"No way," Camilla said. "He's said a hundred times that we're too young for cell phones. Besides, what would we even use them for?"

"Well, they'd come in handy right now. There's no way this thing will fit in my pocket." He looked down at the walkie-talkie in his hand. "See you tonight."

Since Camilla was heading home to probably read a book, I followed Drew to his baseball practice. I'd almost gotten used to jogging next to Drew instead of riding on the

60

bike. For a moment, I closed my eyes to smell the wind. When I opened them, Drew wasn't next to me. He had turned down the street, even though the baseball diamond was right in front of us.

I tilted my head and let out a little whine. Where were we going?

"Hang on, buddy. We're just going to make a pit stop before practice tonight," Drew explained. "We're going to Ryan's first to do a little bit of surveillance." He held the walkie-talkie out in front of him.

I could practically hear the grin in his voice. He was loving this spy work, and he hadn't even really started.

Drew pulled over behind a large lilac bush and parked his bike. He peered around the edges of the bush. Purple flowers dusted his brown hair. He pointed across the street to where a man with a huge belly sat on his front porch rocking chair, a baseball cap pulled down over his eyes.

"That's Donovan," Drew told me. "Ryan's stepdad. I've seen him at school." Drew's voice turned down to a whisper, as if he were talking to himself. "He yelled at the secretary when he brought Ryan in late. Said Ryan didn't finish his morning chores and that work was more important than school. Ryan doesn't like him much."

We watched the house, but nothing seemed to be happening. I grew bored and laid my head on my paws. Then the screen door slammed shut. Ryan barged out of the house, his baseball mitt in hand.

"Where are you going?" Donovan demanded.

"I'm going to practice!" Ryan shouted at him. "Just like I do every Thursday." Ryan stormed down the driveway. "If you cared at all, you would know that!"

"Be back by eight," Donovan gruffed. "I need your help cleaning out the barn."

Ryan didn't answer. Once he hit the sidewalk, he started to jog. Drew hopped on his bike and followed him.

Drew kept his distance as we followed Ryan. Ryan ran slowly, but we made it to the baseball diamond without being spotted. I took my place on the bleachers, enjoying the cool metal on my belly. Drew's team, the Brookhaven

Blue Socks, scattered over the field, playing catch and warming up their arms. I watched Drew lob the ball back and forth with a teammate. I wished a ball would hurdle over toward me. I loved a good game of fetch.

Everyone on the team had a partner except for Ryan. He and the coach threw together.

At the corner of the field stood a little boy, blond haired and tan skinned. I knew it wasn't Mikey, but he looked just like him. I got up and sauntered over to him, sniffing the air, waiting for his scent to reach me. But the scent was wrong. Mikey didn't smell like strawberries and laundry soap. Mikey smelled like trampolines and sprinklers, or at least he used to until he got sick. Then he smelled like alcohol wipes and bleach, the same smell as the hospital.

I stopped where I was and watched the little boy. His hand stretched out to me. It wasn't Mikey, I knew. The same sickness that took my leg took Mikey. Then grief took away the rest of my family. Mikey's parents couldn't stay here, couldn't handle all the memories. They couldn't handle me either. They moved to New York and left me.

The boy's hand was still reaching out for me, but a knot had formed in my stomach. I missed Mikey too much, too much to be reminded of his squealing laughter, of his arms wrapped around my neck, of his fingers scratching my back while he slept soundly. I turned around, not wanting to watch the boy's smile fade, and returned to the bleachers.

When the team took turns at bat, Ryan hit the ball out of the park. If it had been a game, he would have scored a home run. He was definitely the star of the team, and he knew it.

After practice, Coach yelled, "Go pick up the balls!"
The team scattered, each boy searching for the baseballs.

Everyone, that is, except for Ryan.

With a quick glance over his shoulder, he slinked over to the bleachers, next to me. Water bottles, jackets, and baseball mitts littered the bench. His eyes narrowed when he saw me watching him. To my surprise, he started kicking at the mitts, overturning the water bottles, and flinging the jackets onto the ground.

I let out a single bark. It got his attention.

"Hush," he commanded.

I barked again. I didn't have to listen to him; he wasn't my human.

Drew heard the barking and started to come over, but he was still pretty far out. Ryan found what he was looking for: the coach's jacket. He turned the jacket pocket inside out, and out plopped the coach's wallet. He opened it just as Drew arrived.

"What are you doing?" Drew yelled. "Put that back!"

"Get out of here, nosy," Ryan sneered.

"I'm going to tell Coach Jackson," Drew said.

"Shove off," Ryan responded.

Drew raced over to the coach. Coach Jackson listened to Drew, then turned and looked at Ryan, the messy bleachers, and his wallet laid out and open in front of him. Slowly, painfully, Coach Jackson came over and sat down next to Ryan, and, with a wave of his hand, dismissed Drew and me.

Drew's jaws ground together angrily. We stopped at the corner of the street and watched Ryan and Coach Jackson's conversation. They kept it quiet; even I couldn't hear it. Ryan took off his jersey, threw it on the ground, and stomped on it.

"I think he just got kicked off the team," Drew whispered.

To my surprise, instead of going home, Drew pedaled back to Ryan's house. I followed, and we waited behind the same purple lilac bush for Ryan. He showed up a few minutes later. Donovan, Ryan's stepdad, was not happy.

"I told you to be home by eight," he growled. "We're gonna have to work in the dark now, and it's your fault." He gave him a shove toward the barn. "Let me know when you're done."

Ryan shuffled to the barn, throwing his mitt on the ground. A scrap of paper fluttered from his pocket to the ground.

Drew waited until Ryan closed the barn door behind him to sneak over and snatch up the piece of paper. "Time to go home," Drew said. "I don't think he's going anywhere else today."

# Chapter 8

Drew filled Camilla in as soon as we got home. The sun had begun to sink behind the horizon, and she was dressed in her pink pajamas that clashed with her hair. Drew explained to her what had happened, about Ryan attempting to steal from Coach Jackson.

Camilla put her book aside. She chewed on her bottom lip, and her fingers tapped the hard cover excitedly.

"What? What are you thinking?" Drew asked.

"Well, you've got to admit, it looks fishy. Robbing two people in one week?"

"But if he needs the money—" Drew started.

"He's thirteen years old! Why wouldn't he ask his parents?"

"You didn't see his stepdad, Camilla, and I didn't see a mom there at all. His stepdad isn't a great parent, by the look of things. I wouldn't blame him if he were trying to run away."

Camilla's eyes widened. "Run away? A thirteen-year-old can't live on the streets. You think he would do that? Do you think he would rob Frank and Coach Jackson to have money to live on the streets?"

"I don't know what his plan is, but we need to do something," Drew said.

"Well," Camilla said, "we don't have any proof yet. We'll keep an eye on him tomorrow. But we should tell Matt as soon as we can."

Static filled the air as Drew played with the walkie-talkie. "How does this thing even work?" he wondered.

A light on the walkie-talkie turned red. Drew pushed down on the large button on the side. "Matt, Matt. Can you hear me?"

His finger released the button. We waited, but nothing happened. Static continued to ring in our ears.

"Matt? Matt, are you there?"

No answer.

"Maybe he's already gone to sleep," Camilla suggested. "Or maybe the other one doesn't work. We didn't check them before we started using them."

"We'll have to check them tomorrow," Drew said. "And I guess we'll have to wait to tell him about Ryan until the morning. A cell phone would be so nice right now!"

Mr. Walker came home sometime after we three had gone to sleep. He was also gone the next morning before any of us had a proper chance to wake up. The twins slept through his goodbye kisses, but he made a point to do them. He had come in, kissed each of our foreheads, and left before the summer sun had even begun to rise.

Camilla woke up soon after he left. "Come on, Drew. We've got to get going!"

Drew mumbled something incomprehensible in his sleep and rolled over. A small puddle formed on his pillow next to his mouth.

With a mischievous smile, Camilla picked up her pillow and hurled it Drew. "Get up!"

Drew rubbed his eyes but obliged. He sat up and blinked stupidly. "What are we doing today?"

"We need to tell Matt our theory and see what he thinks of it."

I stretched and fumbled my way off her bed. My one hind leg got caught in the blankets, and they ended up on the floor with me. Camilla rolled her eyes as she flung them back on the bed.

"Come on. We need to get Matt. Hurry!" She bounded down the stairs. "You, too, Hopscotch!"

I floundered my way down the stairs. She had already put food in my bowl, which was great. I never complained about food. Scarfing down a Pop-Tart, she tapped her toes impatiently while she waited for Drew to appear. He stumbled down the stairs a few minutes later, dressed and yawning.

Camilla narrowed her eyes at him, but Drew held up his hands in defense. "I had to grab a couple of things." On his back was his blue backpack.

Camilla pressed a Pop-Tart into his hand. "Come on. You can eat on the way."

Drew hauled me up into the basket on the back of his bike. After spinning around a few times, trying to get the perfect blanket arrangement, I lay down and we were off. First stop, Matt's house. I had to enjoy my spot while I could. Matt would take it over as soon as we saw him. My tongue hung out of my mouth, the wind tasting of mowed grass and morning dew.

Madelyn opened the door and let us in. "He's in his room," she said. She stalked back into the kitchen and spooned cereal into her mouth.

Drew wasted no time in explaining what happened with Ryan the day before, including the theory that Ryan robbed Coach Jackson and Frank because he planned to run away. Matt listened, but it was hard to tell what he was thinking since his mouth and nose were covered with a bandana and he had donned his sunglasses. They slipped a little down his nose, revealing the bruise on his forehead that had turned more yellow instead of vivid purple. It was starting to heal.

"I have an idea," Drew said, "but I don't want you guys to freak out."

"That probably means it's going to be crazy," Camilla whispered to Matt. They were sitting on the floor close together, though not touching. I went over and sat between them, forcing them to scoot a few inches apart. I arranged myself into a comfortable position and lay my head on Camilla's lap, pleased with myself.

Drew wasn't paying attention. "The walkie-talkies don't work, so we need to change our game plan. And Frank is the only one who saw the robber, right?"

"Yes," Matt and Camilla answered slowly.

"Do you think we could show him a picture of Ryan and he'd recognize him?"

"Dad said that the robber was wearing a ski mask," Camilla pointed out. "He wouldn't be able to separate him from Hopscotch."

I lifted my head and whined. Comparing me to the bully was a low blow.

"Sorry, buddy," she said, but she didn't sound sincere. She patted my head consolingly.

"What about the height of the robber? Or the weight?" Matt spoke up. "Maybe he noticed something about the robber. If any of it ties back to Ryan—"

"Do you guys know Ryan's height and weight off the top of your head?" Camilla interjected. "It's not like he goes around spouting off his weight."

"No." A sly smile lit up Drew's face. He pulled out a crumpled piece of paper from his pocket. "But I know his height." He handed the paper to Camilla.

Inside was a list of letters and numbers that I couldn't make heads or tails of. Camilla and Matt, though, understood.

"This is ingenious, Drew," Matt commented. "Brilliant."

Camilla read out loud. "Yankee Youth League Tournament. Here it is. Brookhaven Blue Socks, Ryan Lewis: five foot six. Okay, but we have nothing on Ryan except he's a bully. He could still be innocent."

"If he's innocent, I'll give you my half of Matt's money," Drew argued. "I caught him trying to steal from Coach's wallet. That's not innocent. Let's go talk to Frank."

"Even if Ryan is guilty, Dad specifically asked us to stay away from Frank. He doesn't need anyone bringing up those awful memories," Camilla reminded him.

"You are such a goody-two-shoes," Drew mumbled. "That's why . . ." He rummaged around in his bag for a minute, then pulled out a container full of peanut butter cookies. I licked my lips. Maybe I'd get one. "That's why we're bringing him cookies. To cheer him up."

"Please, Cam," Matt begged. "I need to get to the bottom of this. If anyone threatened Madelyn . . . With Mom working all the time and Dad gone, it's just us. And after the drive-by with Spencer's sister, I don't want to risk anything happening to my sister. Please." He placed his hand on her arm.

Camilla chewed on her bottom lip, but she stared down at his hand as if it were gold. Eventually she gave in. "Fine. Let's go."

With a whoop, Drew turned toward the door. Holes ran up and down the door where the locks used to be. Trying to poke his finger through each of the holes, Drew asked, "What happened to all your locks, Matt? There used to be a lot of them, but now there's only the deadbolt."

"Mom made me take them off. She said I was overreacting."

When we reached the front door, Matt opened it, then immediately slammed it shut again. In the split second the door was open, a rusted red truck drove slowly in front of the house.

We watched the truck turn the corner. When it was gone, Drew spoke up. "Come on. Let's go."

I was really starting to miss my basket on the back of Drew's bike. The sooner we found Matt's bike, the better. I had to run alongside their bikes the entire four blocks to the gas station on my three legs. I couldn't wait for this investigation to end.

Police tape still surrounded the store and the parking lot, but there were no officers to be seen. Through the window, an older man, scrawny and hunched over, shuffled from aisle to aisle, picking up the scattered candy bars and spilled sodas.

Drew knocked on the glass door before entering, though a bell jingled our arrival. Frank didn't even look up. "We're closed today."

"We know," Drew responded. "We heard about what happened. We wanted to ask—"

"We wanted to say we were sorry," Camilla said, with an elbow into Drew's side. "And ask if there's anything we can do to help." She dug into Drew's backpack and pulled out the package of cookies. "And these are for you."

Frank's eyes shimmered with tears. "Thanks, kids. I always did like you." He snagged a cookie. "I think there's a bag of jerky that was torn open over there," he pointed to the corner of the store. "If he wants, Hopscotch can have some."

Boy, did I ever want some! I pressed my nose to the ground and searched for the jerky. A mixture of scents filled my nose, mainly dirt, burnt coffee, and a hint of something else. Gravel. BO. I focused on the jerky scent. By the time I found it, Drew had started talking again.

"We were wondering if you could tell us anything about the robber. Maybe his height, or what he looked like?" He held up his hands a few inches above his head, about the height of Ryan Lewis. "Was he about this tall?"

The older man shook his head, then grabbed Drew's hand and stretched it as high as it could go. "More like this tall," he said. "Much taller than you kids."

Camilla whispered to Drew, "If he really was that tall, then there's no way it was Ryan. I told you he was innocent." Then she spoke louder for Frank. "We think the same person who robbed you hurt him," she nodded to Matt, who fingered his temples. "We're looking for tidbits of information."

"Sorry, kiddos," Frank said. "I told the police everything I know."

"Was he wearing gloves?" Drew asked, staring at the handprints on the glass door. "Were the police able to get any fingerprints?

Frank shook his head. "I don't recall 'bout the gloves, but there weren't any unusual fingerprints. Just mine and my employees'."

The twins, silent and disappointed, worked on straightening the shelves. Drew grabbed an exploded can of soda and tossed it in the trash. I mopped up the spilled soda with my tongue. It was there, as I was licking up the last of the Sprite, that I saw something. It gleamed under the candy shelf.

I inched forward, digging my nose under the shelf. With my nose stuck there, I scratched furiously with my one hind leg to get closer to the shiny object.

It was a ring. Dark blue, with a silver gem embedded in it. I grumbled and whined and continued to scratch until Camilla took pity on me.

"What you doing there, Hoppy?" She came over and reached under the shelf. Her fingers closed around the ring. My goal accomplished, I backed out from under the shelf and pulled my ears and face into a smile.

"Looks like a ring," she announced, holding it up for everyone to see.

"Ah, yes," Frank said. "Lots of my employees have those. They were giving them to the graduating seniors at the high school. It's a class ring."

"A class ring," Drew repeated. "I didn't even know there were such things as class rings."

"Oh, yes, they're quite popular. Lots of kids get them," Frank said knowledgeably. "I wonder how that got down there and who's missing it. Most of my employees are gone for the summer, touring Europe or whatever they do before they start their first year of college. I don't know how that would have gotten under there." He scratched his chin.

"We'll take it and put it in the lost and found," Camilla suggested. "There's one at the police station. If someone is missing it, then they can find it there."

"If it belongs to one of my employees, then I think I should keep it here," Frank said.

"No one will know that it's been lost here," Camilla said. "Especially if they haven't been here for a few weeks. The police station really is the best place for it."

Frank shrugged. "Okay. If someone comes looking for it, then I'll know where it is." He grabbed another cookie. "Thanks for your help today, kiddos. Come back when things are open and I'll give you a slushie."

We were just opening the door to leave when Camilla stopped and stared at something on the wall. "Frank, who are these people?"

A corkboard full of photos of teenagers hung on the wall next to the door.

"Oh, those are the employees of the month," Frank explained. "Every month, someone who worked extra hard gets their picture on the wall and a candy bar as a thank-you."

There were four pictures in a row, three girls and one boy. Between two of the girls was a big, missing space, about the size of another photo.

"What happened here?" Camilla asked, pointing to the blank space on the corkboard.

Frank's shoulders sunk. "Ah. That would be Tony."

"Did he die?" Matt blurted out.

Frank shot him a look. "No, he didn't die. He was supposed to be employee of the month. I had gotten his picture taken, even had a candy bar set out for him. But the day I told him, one hundred dollars went missing from the cash register. It was only him and me working that day, and I didn't take the money."

"You think he stole from you?" Camilla asked.

"He says he didn't," Frank muttered. "But I don't know who else it would have been."

The twins thanked him for his time, and I licked his hand to express my appreciation for the jerky that I could still taste on my tongue. It was really good jerky.

As the bell jingled our exit, a squealing sound reverberated across the empty parking lot. A rusted red pickup truck peeled off, darting through the caution tape. We watched it screech around the corner and out of sight. A trail of black tire lines crisscrossed the pavement.

## Chapter 9

The four of us raced to the corner, watching the truck disappear. I howled, barked, and even tried chasing the receding threat. My nerves were on edge. He had come to do something, but what?

Drew's mouth hung open.

"I told you, I told you!" Matt yelled. "That truck has been following me for days!"

"It's not the first time we've seen it," Drew muttered. "We believed you after we first saw it."

Camilla interjected. "There's nothing we can do now. We need to go to the police."

I was the first one to the bikes. A piece of paper flapped against the handlebars. The twins and Matt followed slowly as they discussed their next move.

They were taking too long, and this paper could blow away in the wind. I wished I could read human. I snatched the piece of paper with my teeth and brought it to them. Camilla unfolded it and read.

# LEAVE ME ALONE OR ELSE.

"Well, at least we know we're on the right track," Drew said.

Camilla turned the paper sideways. "Do you think we could get fingerprints off this?"

"Not if he was wearing gloves. And he'd have to be in the fingerprint database, too," Drew said. He grabbed the note and slipped it into his pocket, but his eyebrows furrowed together as he did so. "Wait, what's this?" He pulled out another piece of paper. As he read it, he closed his eyes.

"What? What is it?" Camilla asked. She read over his shoulder.

Thank you for believing in me when no one else did.

"This one is Ryan's. He wasn't trying to steal from the coach. He was leaving a note. And I got him kicked off the team." Drew closed his eyes and pressed his palm to his forehead.

"The handwriting is different, too," Camilla pointed out. "There's no way that Ryan left us the threat. We should definitely go tell Dad what's going on now." She got on her bike. "Besides, the police station is only down the road."

"I agree," Drew said. "Matt, are you coming?"

Matt had been strangely quiet during the conversation.

Matt looked from Drew to Camilla, and then down to me. "I don't know, guys. Maybe it's better to just go home and forget about it."

"Are you serious? What about your bike? If we stop now, you won't ever find it. And what about protecting Madelyn?" Camilla's shock and anger shook her voice.

Drew muttered something under his breath with the words "coward" and "wimp." Matt glared at Drew, then turned with pleading eyes to Camilla.

"I can always get a new bike. And if I back out now, maybe he'll leave us alone."

"You saw or heard something that a criminal wants to keep quiet. If you don't figure out what it was, then you're helping a criminal. And there's no way to know that he won't keep stalking you. You have to continue. For us. For Madelyn."

Matt's voice came out as a whisper. "I can't. Not anymore."

Camilla snapped her jaw shut. "Fine. If you want to stop, then you can stop. Come on, Drew. We'll do it on our own."

Matt reached out to her, but she was already out of reach. "Camilla, wait. It's not that I want the criminal to get away, but he's already threatened us. What if Madelyn's next?"

We had already gotten on our bikes. Camilla started pedaling, leaving the rest of us in the parking lot.

"I've got swim practice, but I'll call you later, okay?" Matt called out.

Camilla didn't answer.

Drew helped me onto my rightful place behind his bike seat. Matt's scent covered my blanket, and I quickly tromped all around it to cover it up. My blanket, my scent. Once I was settled, Drew took off. Pedaling furiously, he caught up to Camilla. "What about our ten dollars?"

"Forget about the money. Let's catch a criminal. But first, let's go fill Dad in and have him look at this note." She pulled out the ring, the ring we had found under a gas station shelf. "We should have Dad take a look at this, too."

The police station was much more organized than the last time we visited. Four desks lined the side wall, with phones ringing and lights blinking. Groups of desks clustered each other, each with a police officer studying a case file or searching databases at each desk.

We made straight for Mr. Walker, who was on the phone at his desk.

"I see. Thank you. We'll investigate this more fully. Uh huh. Bye-bye." He hung up the phone, glanced quickly at us, then proceeded to look at the case file in his hand. "What brings you guys in today?"

Camilla pulled out the folded note. "We found this on our bikes today." She dug out the dark blue ring and held it in her hand. "And Hopscotch found this at Frank's gas station."

Mr. Walker's head snapped up. "I told you not to bother Frank."

"Yeah, but—" Drew started, but Mr. Walker held up his hand.

"I asked you not to bother him because he's going through an ordeal right now. It's not safe to be there. We don't know if the robber will come back."

"We know, Dad, but—"

"Detective Walker!" a woman shouted from across the room. "There's a call waiting for you on line two."

He turned back to us, a vein bulging on his forehead. He didn't get angry often, but his flushing face and thinned lips told me he was angry now. He kept his voice calm, though. "Kids, please. Go back home and stay out of trouble. I'll order pizza for us tonight."

Drew opened his mouth to respond, but Camilla cut in first. She kept her eyes on her feet. "Okay, Dad," she said. "We'll see you tonight. Let's go." Grabbing Drew's hand, she led him to the door.

I followed her, my tail drooping. What a mess. He hadn't even read the note from the bikes, and he didn't seem interested in the ring at all. What were we going to do?

In silence, we trudged out the door to our bikes.

"What happened?" Drew gaped.

I followed his gaze to our bikes. The tires were slashed.

This time, we didn't need the note.

"We need to get home," Camilla said. "Now."

"How did someone slash our tires in front of the police station? Isn't that risky?"

"Not if us finding out the truth is riskier," Camilla disagreed. "We have work to do. And we'll have to do it on our own."

***

"What are we doing back here?" Drew murmured. "Dad told us to stay away. And you *told* Dad that we would."

"Dad wasn't going to help us. We're going to have to help ourselves."

Camilla wheeled her broken bike to the backside of the gas station. "Come on," she beckoned Drew. "We don't want the thief to know that we're here again."

Drew followed Camilla and hid their bikes behind some bushes. Standing with her hands on her hips, Camilla examined the area. Her eyes stopped on a camera on the backside of the store.

She stomped across the grounds and barged in the front door, Drew scampering behind her, trying to catch up.

"Hi, Frank," she said. "I noticed there's a camera in the back. It didn't catch anything from the night of the robbery, did it?"

Frank didn't even seem bothered that we had returned so soon. "Just caught a glimpse of the robber is all," he answered. "But he was still wearing a mask."

"Can we see the video?" Drew asked.

"Suppose it can't hurt," the man answered. "If you'll excuse me, though, I think I've seen it enough to last a lifetime. Especially that gun."

"We understand completely," Camilla said, and Frank led us to a back room. Boxes of unpacked candy and bottles of soda lined the walls. In the middle of the room stood a small desk with a computer.

Frank wiggled the mouse and the black computer screen turned to blue. He clicked on a file and pushed the triangle button. "Come on out when you're done," he said as he shuffled past.

We watched for what seemed like forever. Nothing was happening. There was nothing to see in the back of the gas station except for an occasional car driving past.

I suppressed a yawn and let my eyelids droop just a little. Drew and Camilla stared intently at the screen.

"Look!" Camilla pointed to the screen. Matt had pulled up, but his back was to the camera. He hopped off his green bike, and his fingers fumbled at the lock.

But he wasn't the only one there. A tall, gangly person wearing a ski mask suddenly streaked past. Matt jerked his head up, but the robber was back. He had a large tree branch in hand, and as fast as lightning, he brought the branch down on Matt, who crumpled to the ground.

The robber grabbed the bike and pedaled off.

Camilla paused the video. Drew's mouth hung open. "I guess we know what happened to Matt's head," Drew finally said.

"Hold on a second," Camilla said. She skipped the video back a ways and paused it where the robber had a tree branch in his hand.

"Oh, come on," Drew said. "Do we really need to see that part again?"

"Can you zoom in here?" Camilla asked, ignoring her brother's question.

Drew scoffed. "Of course I can." He scooted Camilla's chair over and pulled himself in front of the computer.

*Click, click, click.* Seconds later, the man in the ski mask took up the entire screen.

"Perfect," Camilla said. "Now, slide it over to his hand."

Drew followed Camilla's request, until a large, calloused hand encircling a tree branch filled up the screen.

"There. Stop." Camilla pointed at the hand. "Do you see what I see?"

"He's not wearing gloves," Drew responded, "and he has a bruise on his pointer finger."

"It's the same guy  we met at the library," Camilla said. "The one who didn't like Hopscotch."

"I've got a plan," Drew said.

## Chapter 10

The grass laid flat from our pacing feet. We had been at the park for three hours. I was hot, tired, and thirsty. I gave up pacing and sank beneath an oak tree, enjoying its shade.

"Do you think he's going to come?" Camilla asked.

"If you had asked me two hours ago, I would have said definitely. But now I'm starting to question it," Drew responded.

Drew's plan was actually clever. He had made a fake social media profile, using a picture of me sporting sunglasses, and joined the high school's group page. In a public post, he wrote:

I found a ring at the gas station on Main Street. Meet me at Mack Park at 2:00 if it's yours.

There had been several comments asking who we were, since Drew's account name was Andy Skywalker, a mix between his name and the name of his favorite *Star Wars* character. Drew, though, refused to answer any of them.

And so we had spent our afternoon waiting in the unforgiving sun, ignoring their dad's directions. Not only that, but it was dinnertime. My stomach rumbled as I thought about the pizza Mr. Walker had promised. He'd be home, and we wouldn't be. Gulp. I hoped nothing bad came from this.

Then we saw it—the red truck pulling into the parking lot. I jumped to my paws and watched a gangly young man start toward us.

"Nicely done, Drew," Camilla said.

Drew, though, seemed anxious. His hands clenched into fists. "He'll know," Drew continued. "If he's the thief, he'll know who we are. He'd have recognized Hoppy's picture, and he'll recognize us."

"Hey, punks!" the teen shouted. "Are you the clowns with my high school ring?"

Drew stepped forward, in front of Camilla. "Let me handle this," he whispered to her. He waited for the guy to get closer, then he held out the ring. The silver gem in the middle sparkled in the sunlight. I took my place next to Drew.

"Is this your ring?" Drew taunted. "You'll never guess where I found it."

"Give it to me." The boy was getting closer. His scent was getting stronger. Oil, cement, gravel, and dirt, just like before. He'd probably just gotten off work.

"I think I should actually turn it in to the police. I wonder what they'd say about it being found at the place that just got robbed."

He stepped closer and closer. "Give me the ring. Now."

"What's your name?"

"Give me the ring." His voice came out like a growl, threatening.

I matched his growl with my own.

"Let's just take it easy," Drew said, putting his hand on my back. "Let's just all take it easy."

"I need that ring."

"We get it. You want the ring. Just calm down, talk with us, and we'll give you the ring back."

Camilla jerked her head to Drew. I understood the thoughts that must have been blazing through her head. *The ring is the only evidence we have!*

Drew didn't look at his sister.

"What is it you want to know?"

"First of all, what's your name?"

"Tony. Tony Lochlin."

"And you just graduated Brookhaven High," Drew said.

"Yes," Tony answered through clenched teeth. I heard his heartbeat start to pick up. His patience wasn't going to last for long.

Drew gestured to the rusted red truck. "You've been following us. Why?"

"I haven't been following *you*. I've been following your friend. The nosy one."

Camilla folded her arms. "Then why slash *our* tires? He wasn't with us at the police station. So we'll ask again. Why?"

"I think we're done with this chat. Give me my ring."

The sun was beginning to lower in the sky. We'd been here way too long. Mr. Walker was going to be ticked. And I was hungry. I wondered if there would be any bacon on the pizza.

"Answer the last question, then the ring is yours," Drew stated. Camilla shot him another deadly glare that he valiantly ignored. "Why were you following Matt?"

I watched Tony's chest rise and fall. I would give him to the count of five before I pressed him for the answer. One. Two. C. Eleven. Five. I prepared my most fearsome bark, allowing it to grow in the back of my throat.

"Let's just say he was somewhere he wasn't supposed to be."

"And where was that? The gas station?"

"I answered your questions. Give me my ring." His brown eyes seared with anger. He clenched his fingers into fists.

Holding out his hand, Drew said, "Sure. No problem." The ring rested calmly on his palm.

In a blink, Tony snatched the ring and left.

We watched his receding figure.

Camilla's red hair whacked her face as she whipped her head around. "What did you do? You just gave away our best piece of evidence!"

"Yes," Drew said. "But now we his name, and probably where the bike is." He rubbed his hands together mischievously, a smile creeping on to his face. "And tonight, we're gonna go get it."

***

Despite being pizza-without-bacon night, dinner was a quiet affair. Mr. Walker hadn't even returned home from work when we arrived, which we were all grateful for. Although our stomachs complained loudly from the lack of food, the twins did little more than sip their root beer and nibble their pizza.

If the pizza had had bacon, I would have scarfed it down.

"What did you guys do today?" Mr. Walker asked the twins.

"Nothin'. Went to the park," Drew answered. He didn't look at his dad.

"I'm sorry I shooed you out of the station today. Did you get everything you needed?"

"Just wanted to say hi," Camilla said. She didn't look at him either, and her voice sung with annoyance.

Mr. Walker stopped trying to have a conversation.

Whether because of nerves for their upcoming mission, or because their feelings really were hurt about how he had blown them off earlier, they quietly said their goodnights. Before I followed them up the stairs, I snuck a glance at Mr. Walker, who sat at the table with his head in his hands. Part of me wanted to go comfort him, but the other part of me knew the twins needed me, too.

After a while, I heard Mr. Walker switch off the lights in the kitchen and start up the stairs. We pretended to be asleep. Camilla clutched the picture of her mother, and Drew turned to face the wall, his back to the door. I rested near Camilla's feet.

Mr. Walker came in, gave each of them a kiss on the forehead, rubbed my head, then retired to his room.

The hours passed on. At some point, I did drift off to sleep. The padding of Drew's feet woke me up. Camilla sat up in her bed and watched her brother.

"Are you sure about this?"

"I pulled up his address from the phone book. He doesn't live too far." He looked down at his palm. Black letters stained his hand.

"Even with our bike tires slashed?"

"It's just a few blocks. We'll be back in twenty minutes. Dad won't even know we're gone."

Camilla gulped audibly. "What about the ring?"

"We'll grab that, too. Shouldn't be hard. Sneak in, grab the ring, grab the bike. One of us can ride it back. We'll stick it in the garage until morning, then return it to Matt."

Camilla rolled her eyes. "There are so many issues with this plan. What if Tony's doors are locked? What if the bike isn't in the garage? What if we wake up Dad?"

A shrug was his answer. "We'll make it work. Come on."

Drew was dressed in all black, complete with a beanie that covered his already dark hair. His fingers were hidden in winter gloves. An inch of skin showed on his wrist.

Butterflies fluttered in my stomach. Breaking into someone's house was more than I had bargained for, and more than the twins had expected, I'm sure. I thought about Mr. Walker at the table after dinner and how disheartened he looked. Maybe I should wake him and stop them from going out.

"Maybe we should just try telling Dad again about the note and the ring," Camilla said.

"No way. You said yourself that we have to do it on our own."

I watched as Camilla sifted through her thoughts. Her face changed from nervous, to hurt, to determined.

"Let's go," she finally said.

Drew slid the window open and crept onto the roof outside the window. He grabbed the ledge, then lowered himself slowly, landing on all fours like a cat. Watching his performance, Camilla rolled her eyes.

"Come on, Hopscotch. We're taking the stairs."

I was grateful for that. My three legs wouldn't handle the drop that well, and I didn't trust Drew to catch me.

"You're ruining the fun," Drew complained when we met him outside.

"At least we aren't going to break our legs," Camilla countered.

"I didn't break my leg," Drew grumbled.

The streetlights illuminated our figures as we snuck up to a shabby, run-down house. "This is it," Drew told us.

Cars piled around the outside, the grass was overgrown, and vines snuck up the sides of the house. It looked like a death-trap.

"How are we going to get in?" Camilla hissed.

"I hadn't thought of that," Drew replied, sheepishly. "Look for open windows. It's hot out here tonight. Maybe he left one open."

The twins scoured the house. There was no open window. Drew tried the handle on the front door. Locked.

I hobbled around, sniffing. There wasn't much to smell: no dog scents, no cats (thankfully). It was then that I caught the faintest of scents—a hint of chlorine, like Matt, and rubber. His bike. I sniffed harder, following the trail. It led me to the unfenced backyard, and to the back door, where the trail ended.

My nose bumped into the door, but to my surprise, a part of the door swished open. A doggie door. A grin crept onto my face. I snaked through the doggie door, listening closely for any sounds from within and wincing at the sounds of breaking twigs and hoarse whispers. The twins were louder than they thought.

After making sure that the only sounds from the house were snores and steady breathing, I slinked to the front of the house. The front door had a dead bolt. Proudly, I raised myself onto my one hind leg, placed my front two paws on the door, then turned the bolt with my nose. A satisfying *click* told me my job was accomplished: the front door was unlocked.

I scratched softly at the door.

"Was that Hopscotch?" Camilla whispered.

"It must have been. But where is he?"

I scratched again.

Camilla's footsteps came to the front door. "I already tried that," Drew told her.

She twisted the knob anyway, and the door opened. I stood there, beaming at her, my tail wagging happily. For a second, she stooped down and rubbed my ears. "Good boy, Hopscotch," she said.

Drew followed behind her. "I'll go find the ring. You get the bike."

"What happens if Tony wakes up?" Camilla asked.

A long, heavy snore echoed from down the hallway. "I don't think he will," Drew replied. "Meet me outside." With that, he tiptoed toward the sound of the snores.

Camilla and I watched him for a second before we blindly made our way to the garage. The house was a disaster. Clothes, pizza boxes, and soda cans littered the floor. Every step Camilla took sounded like an avalanche. Camilla groped at the walls, fumbling in the darkness, not daring to turn on the light. Finally, we found the garage and entered. Camilla closed the door behind us, then risked turning on the light.

We blinked in the brightness. On the other side of the cluttered garage stood a bright green bike.

"There it is," Camilla whispered.

Camilla tiptoed to the bike, then hoisted it over her shoulder and carried it back to me. "I don't dare open the garage in case it wakes up Tony," she murmured. Especially since Drew is in there."

She rolled it out the front door, me following behind her. "He'll meet us out here," she said more to herself than to me. "We'll wait for him."

We waited. And waited some more. The moon began to creep back toward the horizon. Where was Drew? What was taking him so long?

"We need to go in after him," Camilla finally said. "He's taking too long."

She pressed the door open. "Drew?" she whispered. "Drew!"

No answer.

The house was quiet. The snoring had stopped.

We crept down the hallway. A door hung open, a sliver of moonlight shining through. Silently, Camilla opened the door a little wider. Drew stood next to the bed, staring at Tony, who was still asleep. He put his fingers to his lips and pointed down at Tony. There around his neck, shining in the last of the moonlight, was the class ring.

Now we knew what was taking Drew so long: he couldn't get the ring.

Camilla shook her head. *Don't try it*, she seemed to say. Drew gazed fiercely at the ring. After a moment, he stepped back to the edge of the room, next to the open closet. Camilla and I tiptoed into the room and met him there.

"I know what you're thinking," Camilla breathed. "Don't do it."

"I can get it," Drew argued. "I can get the ring."

"No," Camilla disagreed. "You're going to get us all caught."

The lights overhead flashed on. It blinded me for only a second. At the bedroom door Tony stood, awake, shirtless, and glaring at us.

I didn't have time to react. He flew across the room and shoved us in the closet, slamming the door shut.

Camilla wiggled the doorknob. It didn't budge.

We were trapped.

## Chapter 11

It was my fault. I should have seen or heard him coming, but I was too focused on the argument. Too focused on the ring. Too focused on everything that wasn't Tony Lochlin himself.

"As long as you're locked in there, you might as well listen," Tony said through the door. "There will be no screaming, no kicking the door, no misbehavior at all."

"Our dad will find us, you know," Camilla spat.

"He knows where we are," Drew added.

Tony barked out a laugh. "Oh, he does, does he? He lets you wander the streets at night, breaking into houses? I doubt it. You snuck out. He won't know you're missing until morning, and by then I'll be long gone."

I shoved my nose under the door. Pounding footsteps and slamming drawers told me everything I needed to know. He was packing. He was making good on his word and leaving.

"And what? You're just going to leave us here?" Camilla demanded.

"Yup," came his response.

Camilla heaved a frustrated sigh and slammed her fist against the door. "Let us out of here!"

Her fist banged again on the door. It shook under her rage and panic. "Let us out. Let us out!"

The footsteps stopped.

Except for Camilla's banging and screaming, it was quiet. Scarily quiet.

We needed to quiet her down, and fast. I didn't trust what Tony would do if we made too much noise. I shimmied over to Camilla and nudged leg with my nose, softly but sternly. Her knees sunk to the ground and she wrapped her arms around my neck.

Drew moved to the door. The lights from the room through the slats in the door made white slashes on his ninja outfit. "Why'd you do it, Tony? Did the hundred dollars give you everything you needed?" he asked through the door.

Tony scoffed at that. "A hundred dollars? At the end of the workday, do you know how much money is in that register? Close to a thousand dollars! That's enough for me to get out of this worthless town and get a start somewhere else, somewhere big. Somewhere I should have been in the first place."

"'In the first place'?" Camilla asked. "What do you mean?"

I heard Tony grind his teeth together from the other side of the closet door. "It was Frank's fault. I'd done nothing, *nothing!*" He grunted and a *bang* echoed through the house.

"Frank couldn't come by to help me close the shop; it wasn't a big deal. I'd closed the shop down many times before. There was a group of teenagers outside, a few years younger than me. I thought nothing of it. They didn't seem to be doing any harm. Frank always asked us to leave the money in a box in the store, then lock the store and drop the keys off in his garage.

"So that's what I did. I slipped *all* the money inside the metal box, then hid it underneath the counter. I locked the door behind me and walked over to Frank's to drop the keys off in his garage. I was done for the day and already clocked out at work, so I wasn't getting paid for taking the keys to Frank.

"The next morning, Frank called me in to work even though it was my day off. I didn't know anything had happened. He told me that a hundred dollars was missing from the register. Only he and I had worked that day." He swallowed. When he spoke again, Tony's voice raised a couple of pitches. "He fired me. I was saving up for college, and he fired me. No one else would hire me since they thought I was a thief.

"I didn't steal that one hundred dollars. One of those teenagers I saw? He was Frank's nephew. He had a key to Frank's house, and I bet he used the key to get into the garage to get the key to the money. Because it wasn't me.

"Frank might have been short a hundred dollars, but now I was down thousands of dollars because of something that I didn't do. I didn't have any other way to go to college. Now I'm stuck at a job I hate, saving up more money to try to go to college. It's not fair. So I took what he had from the cash register. Insurance would pay him back; they are prepared for thefts and stuff. Then I can go to college—get out of this small town and make a name for myself."

"You've already made a name for yourself," Drew butted in. "As a thief."

"Not yet, I haven't. No one else knows what happened except you and me."

"What are you going to do with us?" Camilla asked from underneath me. Her voice sounded stronger, more determined.

A laugh sounded from the room. "You said your dad knew you were here. You won't be in there too long, will you?" He continued laughing.

Drew and Camilla exchanged a look. It seemed they had no ideas, and neither did I. But I had to come up with one, fast.

Then it hit me.

I whined and moaned emphatically, shuffling around the closet, sniffing the floor. Drew and Camilla did nothing but stare at me. Based on their reactions, I'd have to work it a little harder.

My cries climbed higher, shriller. They became yelps as I scratched the closet door. I scratched faster and yelped louder.

"Make him shut up," Tony growled. Through the slits in the closet door, I saw the neighbor's light turn on. My plan was working.

Drew's face lightened with understanding. He rapped on the door with his fists as I continued to scratch. "He needs to go outside!"

"No he doesn't," Tony snapped. "Make him be quiet."

"He needs to go to the bathroom. Unless you want that all over your floor . . ." Drew trailed off. "He won't make any more noise if you take him to the bathroom."

The closet door burst open. "Fine," Tony snarled. "Come on, dog. Let's go."

He yanked on my collar. I held my ground, waiting for the perfect moment. Again he pulled, but I took a step back. The collar slid right off my neck. Perfect. With one last howl, I raced through the house, to the back door, and through the doggie door. With a curse, Tony chased after me.

After a quick lap around the yard—without stopping to go to the bathroom—I charged back into the house. Tony was fast on his two legs, but I was faster on my three. I raced back inside, Tony only a handful of steps behind me.

During my diversion, Drew and Camilla had scrambled into the kitchen and dialed 911 on the landline. The line rang through once, twice. Tony stormed into the kitchen, his face twisted in anger.

"911, what is your emergency?" a woman's voice spoke from the phone.

Tony stepped forward. "Hang up the phone." It was a threat.

Drew matched Tony's advance. I stood next to Drew, ready to spring. A mere three feet separated us.

Camilla whispered hurriedly behind us. "We're at 2191 North Maple Drive. We've been kidnapped. Please hurry!"

"Officers are on their way." Her voice was amazingly calm for this situation. No one in the kitchen felt as calm as her voice was. "Stay on the phone with me until they get there."

The woman's voice, although calm and assured, carried over to Tony. Tony's face dripped sweat, his eyes widened, and his hands shook. The police were coming to his house, and he had a policeman's kids in his house.

For a moment, he stood there staring at us, frozen. Then, in a flash, he was gone. I hadn't expected him to run, and his snap decision caught me off guard. But I had no time to lose.

I sped off after him. I wouldn't let him get away, not after what he'd done to Matt and Frank, and especially not after how he'd locked Drew and Camilla in the closet.

Tony darted into his bedroom and grabbed his backpack from the bed. A black sock hung out of the zipper. He turned to see me blocking the door. Without hesitating, he slid the window open and dived into the bushes below him. I leaped through the open window, too, continuing to dash after him. Dogs' eyes aren't as good as cats' eyes in the dark, but they're better than humans'. Tony wasn't on the road or the sidewalk; he was sprinting from yard to yard, then darting behind bushes, flower pots—anything that would give him cover.

Sirens whirred in the background.

I *would* catch Tony. I didn't know what I was going to do when I caught him, but I'd worry about that later. Right now, I just needed to make sure he didn't get away. Each of my pawsteps drummed in my ear. They were too loud. I veered onto the grass to quiet them. No matter what I did, though, I couldn't quiet the pounding of my heart in my ears.

The police cars and their flashing lights sped right past us. Mr. Walker's car was in the lead. The cars screeched to a stop outside of Tony's house. I paused my chase for a moment to watch Drew and Camilla run into their father's arms.

They were safe.

I continued, stealth mode now, on Tony's trail. My moment of celebration caused me to lose sight of him, but I could still smell his scent and hear the pounding of his footsteps in the rustling grass.

Turning the corner, I saw him: he stood at the edge of a yard, in front of a car. He wiggled the handle and fell into the driver's seat. I picked up my pace, not caring about the noise. Then an idea hit me. Noise! The memory of Mr. Walker stumbling to work in the middle of the night danced in front of my eyes.

I howled and barked for all I was worth as I charged to the stationary car. It wouldn't be stationary for long if I didn't hurry. My howls rang through the air, and they didn't go unanswered. Soon, every dog on the street returned my howls and my barks, yipping, yapping, growling, and barking. Mayhem ensued. Even as I ran past, lights blinked on in several houses, and many silhouettes appeared to be talking on the phone. Perfect.

The car that Tony had broken into rumbled to life just as I reached it. I vaulted all seventy pounds of myself on top of him, sending him flying backward. I pinned him to the seat, glaring down at him, raising my lips in a dangerous growl.

The chorus of barking surrounded us. Tony's eyes darted left and right, then landed on his backpack. His hand twitched to move toward it, but I let out a threatening bark. Tony remained motionless, staring at my bared teeth.

The song of sirens started up again. The neighborhood dogs hadn't given up their endless howling, for which I was grateful. A police car screeched to a halt, followed by several more, surrounding us. I remained where I was, glaring at the criminal.

"Hopscotch," a voice said. "Let him go."

I growled in response.

A soft hand rested on my back, then trailed up to my ears. "Come on, Hopscotch," a different voice said. "Dad's got him. Let's go home."

I tilted my head slightly, still keeping an eye on Tony but also trying to see who was talking. A flash of red hair caught my eye. Camilla.

"Come on, Hopscotch. We're safe. Let's go."

I surveyed the scene. Multiple police officers stood around us, and Mr. Walker had knelt next to me, handcuffs in his hand. Detective Mills, Mr. Walker's new partner, stood behind him with her hand on his shoulder.

"You did good, boy," Mr. Walker said to me. "You did good. Let me take over."

I backed out of the car and out of the circle of police. Camilla and Drew threw their arms around my neck. My fur was soon wet from Camilla's tears.

Mr. Walker snapped his handcuffs around Tony's wrists. Detective Mills grabbed Tony and hauled him up. "I got him, Ken. I'll take him in."

Mr. Walker nodded his thanks. He threw his arms around each of the twin's shoulders and said, "Come on, you three," Mr. Walker said. "Let's get you home."

## Chapter 12

"I know you're not asleep," Mr. Walker stated as he walked into the twins' room. He carried a small gift bag in front of his chest. It was afternoon, and while the twins and I did sleep for a long time, we had also been awake for a long time and pretending to be asleep when Mr. Walker came in.

Camilla sat up and hugged her knees to her chest. Drew was still facing the window, his back to us.

Mr. Walker approached Drew first. "Come on, bud. Sit up and talk to me."

Drew didn't budge.

"It was my fault," Mr. Walker continued. "I'm sorry."

Drew sat up and turned. "We came to you because we needed you, and you blew us off. You didn't even listen to us."

"Tony had left us a note," Camilla added. "He threatened us, and you didn't listen."

Mr. Walker grabbed each of their hands. "I've learned from my mistake," he said. "I've never, ever been more scared than when I woke up and you weren't here. And then there was the call from work saying there was a kidnapping."

I studied his face and took in the creases that had formed around his eyes since the night before.

"I will never do anything that jeopardizes our relationship again," he promised. He grabbed Drew's chin and gently pulled it up. "I promise."

Drew swallowed and nodded.

"Next," Mr. Walker continued, "that was the bravest thing I've ever seen. But I have to know, is this mystery-solving thing going to become a habit?"

Drew muttered unintelligibly under his breath, and Camilla shrugged.

Mr. Walker sighed. "If it's going to become the new norm, then I think we need to set a few ground rules. If it's not . . ."

"You mean we can keep doing it?" Drew interjected. "You're not mad at us?"

"I'm not mad about you helping your friend. I *am* mad about you sneaking out in the middle of the night," he said sternly. "That must never happen again. Agreed?"

Drew nodded as he stared at his lap.

Camilla held out her pinky for Mr. Walker. "Pinky promise," she said.

With a smile, Mr. Walker handed them the gift. Ribbons and scraps of tissue paper soon littered the floor.

I sunk my head down onto my paws. He forgot about me again.

"Here, boy," Mr. Walker said. "I haven't forgotten about you." With a rub of the head, Mr. Walker handed me a package from his jacket pocket.

Jerky. My tail thumped against the edge of the bed as I nosed the jerky. Mr. Walker opened the bag for me and handed me several pieces. I was munching on my first piece when Drew exclaimed, "No way!"

In his hand, he held a small device. It was dark gray and buzzed when Drew held down a button. On the back was a series of numbers. Camilla glanced at them once, and I knew she had already memorized the numbers.

"The phone has GPS," Mr. Walker said. "So I'll be able to track you down if you get lost or," he winced, "kidnapped again."

Drew flung his arms around Mr. Walker. "Thank you, thank you, thank you!"

"There's one more thing in there," Mr. Walker said.

Digging her hand into the bag, Camilla withdrew a compact box. Camilla's mouth hung open as she stared at it. I examined the contents. Inside the little black box with a handle was a pamphlet. Camilla read it out loud.

# Detective Kit

# A Guide to Becoming a Detective

Inside, a pair of binoculars, a magnifying glass, a notepad, fingerprint powder, and caution tape fit neatly and compactly.

"This is totally wicked!" Drew exclaimed. Within minutes, the contents had been unwrapped and spread out on Camilla's bed.

Drew's fingers snatched up every item. He'd bring it close to his face and examined it, ooh-ing and ahh-ing, especially as he examined the fingerprint powder.

"And," Mr. Walker continued, "I have a new case for you two."

Drew jumped off the bed and hurled questions at his father. "Who? What happened? Did someone else get robbed? Are they going to pay us?"

"Hold on." Camilla grabbed Drew's arm and yanked him back onto the bed. "We still need to return Matt's bike. Unless you need it for evidence, Dad?"

"Nope, we have what we need. Take your phone with you."

I sniffed at the bag of jerky wistfully, then followed Drew and Camilla out the door.

In the front yard sat Matt's green bike. It shone brilliantly like it was new. Mr. Walker must have washed it while we were inside sleeping.

Camilla rode Matt's bike over, and Drew and I followed on his bike. Camilla rang the doorbell as the sun sank behind the hills. I greeted Matt with a large lick when he opened the door. "Hey, Hopscotch. Who's a good boy?" His fingers scratched my back.

He turned to Drew and Camilla. "I heard what happened," he said. "It was all over the news. Are you two okay?"

"We got your bike," Camilla said, shyly. She tucked one foot behind the other while fiddling with a strand of her hair.

Matt blinked. "You did it? You found the bike?"

"We saw you at the gas station on Frank's security footage. You were there just as Tony was leaving. He hit you over the head with a branch and stole your bike as a getaway vehicle."

"Wow, you guys. You did more than I ever expected." He slid his wallet out of his pocket and handed them the ten-dollar bill.

Drew snatched it from him, but catching Camilla's eyes, he said, "Thanks for trusting us, Matt. We're glad we could help." He dutifully returned the money.

As we began to leave, Camilla said, "I'll be right behind you, Drew."

Drew looked from Matt to Camilla, then shook his head. He took the hint, though, and waited by the bike.

"Camilla . . ." Matt started.

She met his eyes, waiting.

"I—well, you—um . . ."

"Can I come in?"

He stepped back and let us in. "Hi, Camilla," Madelyn said. She was curled up in an armchair, reading a book.

Matt led Camilla and me back to the kitchen, offering her some lemonade. She shook her head, but pulled up a seat.

"Listen," she said, "I'm sorry about how I reacted earlier. I was frustrated, and scared, and I didn't understand—"

"I should have listened to you," Matt said. "If I had, then maybe you wouldn't have been kidnapped."

"If—if you want to, I'd love to take you up on your offer of talking sometime," she said. The color of her cheeks matched her hair.

"I'd love to," he answered immediately. He flushed slightly, then leaned forward and kissed her cheek. "And thanks." He took a step back, staring at his feet.

Camilla's mouth opened, but no sound came out at first. When she regained the ability to speak, she said, "We got a phone. I'm sharing it with Drew, but if you want to . . ." She reached for a pen on the counter and scribbled the number on the back of his hand. "You can reach me here. See you around."

Her face flurried a mixture of pride, embarrassment, and delight. I nudged her hand with my head as we left Matt's house.

"Don't say a word," she muttered when she saw Drew.

Drew made a face. "I don't want to know about your sappy love life." He climbed on his bike. "You go ahead and head home. I have one more stop I need to make. Hoppy, you coming with me?"

With a yap, I made ready to jump up onto the back of his bike. "Whoa, whoa, whoa. Easy. Wait for me." Drew came around and hauled me up onto my normal spot. I settled into my basket, fluffing up the blanket before lying down. "See you at home, Cam!"

I enjoyed the evening breeze blowing in my ears, but it didn't last long. We were at the baseball diamond. Coach Jackson was loading up the last of the baseballs and bats into the back of his truck.

"Coach!" Drew yelled, waving his arms in the air. "Coach, I gotta talk to you!" He pedaled his bike faster.

Coach Jackson turned, his face unreadable through the sunglasses and the baseball cap pulled down low. Leaning against the fence, he waited for us.

Drew came to a stop in front of him, panting.

"Easy there, tiger," Coach Jackson said. "Catch your breath. What's going on?"

Drew held up a finger, indicating for him to wait. He rummaged around in his pocket until he withdrew a slip of paper. It was crumpled up, but I recognized it immediately; it was the paper that Ryan had thrown on the ground after being kicked off the team.

I listened to the conversation as I stared at the little boy on the baseball diamond. It was the same boy I had seen at Drew's practice. Now that I saw him closer, I recognized who he was. He was Coach Jackson's son. His mischievous blue eyes and his jubilant smile were the spitting image of his father.

"I was wrong," Drew said between gasps, "about Ryan. He wasn't trying to steal from you. He was leaving you a note." He thrust the note into the coach's hands.

I inched my way onto the field.

"Thanks for bringing this to me, Drew. I know it must have been hard. I'll go talk to Ryan and tell him that he can play this weekend at the tournament."

Drew told me that it was time to go. But I wasn't ready yet. I was still watching the boy on the field throwing the baseball up in the air and swinging the bat at it. He hadn't hit the ball once yet, nor had he seen me. He threw the ball up and swung his bat around, missing yet again. With only a moment's hesitation, I dashed up next to the boy and grabbed the bouncing baseball.

The boy shrieked in delight and made to grab the ball. I pranced away from him, and we started a game of chase. After running to first base and then back to home, I let the boy catch me. I rolled over onto my side, dropped the ball, and allowed the boy to give me a belly rub.

"Charlie!" Coach Jackson called. "Say goodbye. It's time to go home."

"Goodbye, doggie," Charlie said. He planted a kiss on my wet nose. "I love you, doggie."

In a flash, he was gone. I watched Charlie run toward his dad. In that moment, I knew that Mikey still loved me, too, wherever he was. And I would always love him.

Drew was awfully quiet on the ride home. When we went inside, though, he grabbed some leftover pizza and told Camilla where he had gone.

She patted him on the back. "You did the right thing. Even if you don't like Ryan."

Drew scoffed. "No one likes Ryan, but I'm glad that I told the truth. Maybe Ryan will be okay with me now."

"Even if he doesn't, I'm still proud of you. Hey," she said suddenly. "Dad told me about the case he has for us. You want to hear it?"

A sly smile lit up Drew's face. "Let's get to work."

TO BE CONTINUED . . .

# Acknowledgments

They say it takes a village to raise a child, and the same can be said of writing book. There are many people I need to thank.

First, to my dad, who taught me a love of writing from a very young age. I have many memories of him writing, of him telling us children stories.

Second, to my sister who showed me that accomplishing your dreams is possible. Not only was she my alpha and beta reader who shared immeasurable feedback, she helped carve the path that I ultimately decided to follow.

To my niece and nephew who read several versions of this story before I settled on it.